HAIBU

LOST IN NEW YORK

Written by Blake Freeman
with Tara Price

Illustrated by Zoltan Boros and Gabor Szikszai

GRAPHIC ARTS
BOOKS®

Published by Graphic Arts Books
In Association with Admit 1 Studios
Printed in Canada

Distributed by Ingram Publisher Services

Download the Haibu app from your app store to learn more, play more, and read more.

Find all things Haibu at www.haibu.love

This book is dedicated to everyone who dared to dream and then took a chance to turn that dream into a reality.

CONTENTS

MONTOOKA..... 9

THE JOURNEY..... 15

A NEW FRIEND..... 19

POLAR SHIFT..... 27

DRIFTING..... 39

IN A NEW YORK MAYOK..... 43

OUT LIKE A LIGHT..... 53

THE NOT-SO-GREATEST SHOW
ON EARTH..... 61

LIONS, TIGERS, AND BEARS, OH LIE! 71

RALLY THE TROOPS..... 85

PRE-GAME..... 91

THE PLANIMALS..... 101

LITTLE BIG TOPPLE..... 109

HOME..... 129

MEET HAIBU

"Hello, my name is Haibu, and I'm a Mayok, or as most people call us, the 'People of the North.' You say my name like if you were saying hello to a ghost: Hi, Boo!

I live way up north, almost as far north as you can go, in a little place not even on a map, called Montooka. It's a colorful little village, where all the houses are painted brightly. That way we can find them easily when they're covered by snow. I live with my mom, dad, and brother, Amook. Sometimes Amook picks on me, but I don't get angry because I know it's just his insecurities. I'm not exactly sure what that means, but I overheard my parents whispering about it one night.

Anyhaibu . . . ha-ha, did you get what I did there? So, everyone in Montooka lives by the creed 'Be Happy, Be Friendly, Be Family.' I spend most of my days playing and working to be the best I can be at fishing and providing for my family. The problem is, I don't want to just fish! I want to be Haibu the

Adventurer! Haibu the Brave! Haibu the Great! I want villagers all over the world to know my name!

Do you want to know something? They will! Some day, most of the world will know my name, and it's all because, as you're going to find out, I have a very special purpose in life."

MONTOOKA

Haibu was running around the front yard, chasing after the dogs like she was in the middle of a great battle, when a neighbor approached. It was Mr. Toko, one of the elders in the village. He was a great warrior and hunter back in his day, and always took time to talk to the other villagers, especially Haibu.

"Well, hello there, little Haibu," he said.

"Hello, Mr. Toko. I'm protecting the village from these ferocious polar bears!" Haibu yelled.

Mr. Toko looked at the dogs that were climbing all over Haibu and licking her face. "Well, I thank you, and I'll leave you be to save us helpless villagers from those wild beasts!" he said.

"Okay, Mr. Toko, I will save us all!"

Mr. Toko walked off in the snow and Haibu continued to play with her dogs. When Haibu's father and brother appeared from behind the house, they were pulling a sled with several hunting and fishing tools.

Haibu ran over, excited. "Atata! Atata!" she called

to her father.

Kneeling next to Haibu, her father spoke. "What are you up to, my little warrior?"

Haibu knew that they were on their way to go ice fishing. She also knew that fishing was usually left up to the men in the village. But what her father and brother didn't know was that Haibu wanted badly to prove that she could fish just as well as the boys.

Haibu replied, "I want to come fishing with you, Atata."

Haibu's brother, Amook, laughed. "You're too *small*; you couldn't catch your own shadow, much less a fish! You want the village to starve?!"

Amook laughed some more and Haibu shouted back at him, "I could catch a lot of fish! Fish with big mouths, just like yours, Amook!"

Chuckling, her father continued, "Haibu, I need you here. Who else is going to protect the village while I'm gone?"

Haibu frowned. "But Atata, I am ready!"

Father rubbed Haibu's head and said softly, "Soon enough, soon enough."

Haibu was left behind as they disappeared into

the snowy distance.

♥

After stomping through the snow, Haibu entered her house and slammed the door behind her.

"Haibu, would you like to help me with dinner?" her mother called.

"No thank you, Anana." Haibu pouted. "I'm not *big* enough to help." Haibu ran into her room and leaped onto the bed.

Moments later, Haibu's mother walked in and sat down beside her. "Haibu, what is wrong?" she asked.

"I don't want to talk about it, Anana."

"Is this because you wanted to go fishing with Amook and your father?"

Haibu sat up. "Yes! Anana, I am as strong as Amook and as good a fisherman as anyone in this village. If they would only let me—"

Haibu's mother interrupted. "Oh my little Haibu, of course you are. But they are going far out to the ice shelf, where the ocean and the ice meet, and it's quite dangerous. You could fall through the ice or stumble upon a nanuq looking for food. It's just not safe."

Nanuq is the Mayok word for "polar bear." From a very young age every villager was taught to stay far away from them. Besides the weather, polar bears are a Mayok's biggest threat.

But Haibu didn't want to listen. "You think I'm scared of a fluffy ole nanuq, Anana?" She stood up on her bed with her hands in the air, mimicking a bear. "Have you ever seen a nanuq this tough, Anana? Rawr! Rawr!" she growled.

"You are a very scary nanuq. It's been a long day, Haibu. Why don't you rest and I will call you when dinner is ready," her mother said, as she headed back to the kitchen.

Haibu dropped to her bed and muttered, "They'll never understand."

THE JOURNEY

Deep in thought, Haibu reached over and grabbed the Shookia given to her by Mr. Toko and the other village elders when she was younger. A Shookia is a bracelet, made to remind villagers that they can achieve anything they want, as long as they work hard and are true to themselves. It is a beloved piece of jewelry in the village of Montooka. The Shookia is made from yellowish rock crystals, and between each crystal sits a small, brown, flat stone. Each stone has a letter carved on it. On this bracelet, the letters spelled out HAIBU.

Haibu slipped it on her wrist and repeated the mantra that had been passed down for generations, for each person to use their name at the end: *"I can do anything I believe I can do. I can be anything I believe I can be. I can achieve anything I want to achieve. I am Haibu."*

Haibu's eyes opened wide, "I can do this! I'm going to do this! I will show all of them!" She quietly gathered a few things into a backpack and slowly opened the bedroom window for her escape. Quiet as a mouse, she dropped into the snow, brushed herself off, and headed toward the shed in the backyard. As she crept past the side of the house, she stopped to peek into the kitchen window. There she saw her mother still cooking dinner.

Haibu carefully etched a heart into the frost on the window and whispered, "I love you, Anana." Then she sprinted to the shed, where she grabbed the fishing tools and bait and placed them on a sled.

Haibu headed out, pulling the sled loaded with her supplies behind her. Haibu braved harsh weather as she traveled through the snow toward the frozen blue sea. The wind was howling and the snow made it very difficult to see, but she pushed forward.

"Come on! You can do this, Haibu!" she yelled to herself.

After hours of pulling the sled through the fierce storm, sleet and snow stinging her face with every step, Haibu finally reached the place where the land met the sea. She stood on the shallow ice and looked around for her father and brother. They were nowhere to be seen.

"Good!" she thought. "They would just send me home."

With darkness setting in, she began building a snow shelter to keep her safe while she slept. Haibu cut block after block from the snow and stacked them perfectly to make the igloo. This was a difficult task for three villagers, much less one small one like Haibu, but she was determined.

Haibu continued working until the igloo was finished, then crawled in and fell immediately to sleep.

A NEW FRIEND

DRIP. DRIP. DRIP.

The shelter was melting in the morning sun, pulling Haibu out of a deep, dreamy sleep. She woke up full of energy.

"It's time to fish!" she shouted.

No one was around, but the crisp, cold air felt good after her cozy sleep. Emerging from the shelter, Haibu squinted to see the ice shelf in the distance, way up the coast. The ocean waves were gently cresting the edge of the ice, where it met the sea. Standing perfectly still, Haibu took it all in.

"Wow. You are a beautiful world," she whispered. "But I've got no time to stare at you right now. There are fish to be caught!"

CRACK!

Haibu slammed her pickaxe into the ice, over and over and over again until . . .

CRACK!

SPLASH!

The pickaxe broke through the ice and water

splashed out of the hole. "It worked!" Haibu shouted. Haibu knew what she was doing and wasted no time grabbing the fishing pole and bait from the sled.

Almost immediately after dropping in her line, Haibu started pulling out fish after fish after fish. Cheering with excitement, she shouted out to no one in particular, "I knew I could do this! These fish are bigger than Amook!"

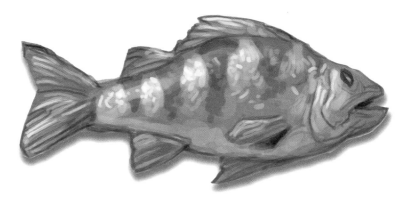

Smiling and laughing to herself and the fish she was catching, Haibu piled each of them neatly on the sled. It was one on top of the other, higher and higher. In no time, the stack grew so high that it was taller than the roof of the igloo! Exhausted, Haibu looked over to the pile of fish and then down at her Shookia bracelet.

"I can do anything I believe I can do," she

whispered. *"I can be anything I believe I can be. I can achieve anything I want to achieve. I am Haibu."* Then she smiled. She felt really good about herself.

Suddenly, Haibu heard a string of thumping noises. The fish she caught were slipping off the sled and spreading all over the ice. Standing where the pile of fish used to be was a small, white, fluffy seal pup with eyes as big as full moons. He looked at her guiltily, knowing he had been caught trying to steal a fish.

Haibu asked, "Now, who might you be, mister?"

The seal lowered his head like he was being scolded.

Haibu pointed at him and then at the fish. "No. Not yours! You better skedaddle, or I will make you into a fur cap!"

The seal turned his big eyes back to Haibu, as if to say he was sorry. That surprised her, and she melted a bit inside. To make the seal feel a little better, Haibu grabbed one of the fish and threw it in front of him. The seal settled in for this snack while Haibu gathered all the tools. When she looked back, the seal was no longer eating the fish. Instead, he was staring intently at Haibu.

"Go on!" Haibu urged. "I gave you a fish! Now eat it and go!"

As Haibu continued to pick up tools, she heard a noise behind her. She spun around to find the seal's face inches from hers. Surprised, but not scared, Haibu dropped the tools just as the little seal planted a big wet kiss right in the middle of her forehead!

Wiping the slobber away, Haibu sternly replied, "No, Mr. Seal! You need to go home!"

That did not happen.

The seal scooted even closer to Haibu's face and smothered her with kisses and more kisses. When he was done, he lay his head on Haibu's shoulder and stared innocently at her with his perfectly round, midnight-black eyes.

Haibu snuggled into him for a moment. It felt good. It made her think of good thoughts. *Be Happy, Be Friendly, Be Family.*

"Okay, fine. You can have another fish if you'd like."

Happily accepting the offer, the seal continued to eat. "You're lucky you're so cute, Mr. Seal. I

wouldn't give just *anybody* my fish. I need these to prove to my family and my village that I am as strong as they are!"

With his head cocked to the side, the seal seemed to be trying to understand all the words that were coming out of her mouth.

"My name is Haibu. What's your name? Nosey? Because you *do* seem a little nosey." Haibu giggled. "Maybe I'll just call you Kanuux," she said, saying the word like Kuh-new. "Kanuux means heart! Your cute little black nose is shaped just like a heart."

The seal nodded at Haibu.

"You like it? Great! That's what I'll call you then—Kanuux! By the way, a heart is my favorite shape, so you are now my favorite Kanuux. Do you want to come home with me? You can help me fish, and everyone in the village will know who we are! The dynamic duo!"

♥

Soon, it was midday, and Haibu had been fishing since early morning, pulling out huge fish that weighed nearly as much as Kanuux the seal. All that work made Haibu exhausted. Likewise, Kanuux was sleepy from all the fish he had eaten. Haibu yawned as loud as a ship's horn. Kanuux's eyelids grew heavy.

Haibu turned to Kanuux with a good idea. "I think we should have a nap before our trip back."

She lay down on the ice and Kanuux lay his head across her stomach, and they both drifted off into their own little dreamlands.

POLAR SHIFT

Haibu's eyes opened suddenly to an unfamiliar crunching noise. Confused, she whispered to herself, "What could *that* be?"

Kanuux was still fast asleep beside her. As Haibu sat up to look around, she was horrified to see a large, full-grown, nine-hundred-pound polar bear just a few feet away. And it was eating all of her fish!

Before she even thought about what she was doing, Haibu screamed at the bear, "Nanuq, NO! Not yours! Shoo!"

The polar bear swung his head in Haibu's direction and snarled, showing his large fangs.

Haibu instantly regretted her actions. "Oh no…"

There are many things for a Mayok to fear in the north, but none more terrifying nor dangerous than an angry polar bear. The ferocious bear lunged straight toward Haibu, stopping directly in front of her! Haibu heard the loud crack of the ice beneath them. She froze.

Growling, the bear showed how tough he was

by flashing his dangerous teeth directly in front of Haibu's face. His growl was so deep that it shook Haibu's entire body, making her teeth chatter and her hair stand up on her arms.

"P-p-please," Haibu begged.

The bear leaned in closer to Haibu and with a voice that sounded like it was coming from somewhere deep, deep, deep in a cave, answered, "Please, what?"

Yesterday was a long day and last night was a short night, so Haibu was more than a little surprised by the polar bear encounter. And now this . . . *Did that polar bear just speak to me? And did I just understand him?*

Haibu wasn't sure what was happening. She wondered if she was in a state of shock. "P-P-Please don't hurt us. Just take the fish."

Now, bears are not known for their manners, nor have they ever been caught using a napkin. The hungry bear leaned even closer, baring his large, razor-sharp teeth and dripping saliva onto Haibu's feet. He roared, "Do you think I need your permission?"

The bear stood on his hind legs, towering over Haibu. Then he crashed back down on all fours and shouted, "I will take what I want, human!"

Needless to say, the crash knocked Haibu to the ground. Kanuux, who was wide awake now, whimpered and scurried backward a few feet. Haibu couldn't take her eyes off of the bear.

She whispered to herself, "He can talk." Slowly, she crawled to her feet, "I'm trying to be nice and offer you fish."

"And I am not asking you for permission! I will take what I want, just like you did!" the bear snarled.

"Then take it and please leave," Haibu shouted back.

The bear began to circle around Haibu. "You humans are weak and pathetic. You take all you can, even when you've had enough."

"I'm not trying—"

"I did not ask you to speak!" the bear roared.

Haibu was terrified. She knew the bear could gobble her up in seconds, then turn around and do the same to Kanuux. Still circling Haibu, the polar bear continued, "You humans are the reason I have to resort to stealing fish. Day and night, I see you pulling fish from the great waters, taking them all with no regard to any other animal out here."

He stopped in front of Haibu and raised a paw in the air. Haibu squeezed her eyes shut, sure this was the end.

CRASH! The bear slammed his paw down on the ice. "You humans are the reason this ice is breaking so easily!" he yelled.

The ice started cracking even more, and this time the sound lasted longer. Haibu looked down, slowly retreating from the sound of the crackling ice. "Not all of us are b-b-bad."

"I know who you are," the bear snarled.

"You do?"

"You're one of those who can speak to animals."

"I am?"

The bear exhaled heavily and poked at Haibu's chest with one of his large claws. "It's a bit obvious, don't you think, human?"

"I don't know. I-I-I've never really tried, I guess."

The bear roared, "That's because your kind doesn't care! It's a good thing only a few of you can talk to us!" The bear roared even louder. Then he turned and began to move away from her, back toward the fish.

"I'm sorry for whatever humans have done to you or your family," Haibu called. She was sincere. She believed in being happy, being friendly, and being family.

The bear stopped short. His head drooped and his low rumbling growl grew louder. He swung around to face Haibu again. "What would you know about my family?"

"N-n-nothing," Haibu stuttered.

"No, you wouldn't understand, because you probably still have your family. How would you feel if I took your family from you?" The bear leaned right into Haibu's face. His breath was so hot she could barely keep her eyes open. "I lost both my cubs to a human like you," he said.

"W-Why?"

The bear leaned within an inch of Haibu's face and gave the loudest roar yet. "So the humans could stay *WARM!*"

The bear raised his paw high in the air once

more, and this time Haibu knew it would be the end. There was no more trying to talk her way out of it. She had to act fast. As the bear swiped, Haibu ducked and rolled under its paw. She dashed to the sled and grabbed the spear. In one motion she spun around and crouched, with the spear pointed towards the bear.

"GO AWAY! I've done nothing to you!" she yelled.

The polar bear leaped closer to Haibu. "I won't give you the chance!" he growled.

Kanuux looked back at Haibu and, with a sad face, dove into the water.

Using every ounce of courage, Haibu started swinging the spear to keep the bear at bay. The size and strength of the polar bear was beginning to set in. It stood tall and let out a deafening roar, then lunged again, striking Haibu in the arm with razor-sharp claws.

"Please stop!" Haibu screamed. "I'm bleeding!"

The bear continued to growl and inch closer and closer to her. "I wonder if my cubs had a chance to say please."

Out of the corner of her eye, Haibu noticed the

Shookia on her wrist. It reminded her of her strength. *I can do anything I believe I can do. I can be anything I believe I can be. I can achieve anything I want to achieve. I am Haibu.* She looked the bear directly in the eyes and shouted, "Not today, nanuq! Today, I am going home and you can't stop me!"

As the bear charged toward her, Haibu rolled under him and jabbed him the leg with her spear. The bear howled in pain. "Enough of this playtime! You're finished, human!"

A cracking noise rose over the howling of the bear and froze them both in their tracks. The sound continued, getting louder and louder.

"It's still going?" Haibu marveled. She knew that a

cracking sound is the last thing any Mayok wants to hear while out on the shallow ice, away from solid land. Haibu knew she needed to get back to the mainland. The ice continued to crack.

"Stop!" Haibu cried. "You're cracking the ice!"

She sprinted toward the land, toward the village, but she heard another crack, and another and another. She felt the ice shift underneath her. The movement caused her and the bear to fall down. Then the worst happened: the ice sheet broke off and separated from the land.

As quickly as the ice broke away from land, a fast current swept it up. It didn't take long for reality to set in. Haibu was stranded on a chunk of ice with an angry polar bear and they were drifting toward the deep ocean.

Crawling to his feet, the bear snarled at Haibu, "I'm going to end this NOW!" He galloped toward her.

"I said, not today, nanuq!" Haibu sprinted toward the bear, full steam.

As if it were planned, they both jumped in the air, the bear roaring and Haibu yelling, "Aiyeeeee!"

Just as they were about to collide, Kanuux leaped out of the water. With one quick motion, he swung his tail flipper into the bear's head, knocking him over onto the ice, into an uncontrolled slide towards the water.

"Kanuux!" Haibu yelled. "You saved me!"

Once in the water, the bear swam back towards Haibu and the floating ice. Haibu knew she couldn't let him back on the ice, so she pointed her spear at the bear to keep him from climbing back on.

"I don't want to hurt you! Go home, leave us alone!" Haibu yelled.

The polar bear tried to climb up, but Haibu slammed her spear close to his paws, persuading him to leave.

"I told you! I don't want to hurt you! Swim back while you can!" Haibu shouted.

The bear began swimming back to the mainland. "This isn't over, human!" he shouted.

Exhausted after the ordeal, Haibu and Kanuux collapsed against each other. Lying on the ice, Haibu noticed that they were drifting farther and farther away from the mainland.

"What will we do, Kanuux?" Haibu asked. "There's no more food, and all of our tools are back on the mainland. If I try to swim, I will freeze before I could make it back to the village." Haibu looked down at Kanuux. "Wait, can you talk too?"

Kanuux didn't say a word; he just stared back at Haibu.

This was a perilous situation.

Haibu and Kanuux were drifting closer and closer to where the water was warmer. Warmer water meant melting ice, and being lost at sea with killer whales was no place for a small Mayok and a baby seal. Haibu fought back tears as she stroked her Shookia on her wrist.

Bringing her arms close to her body, Haibu gently rubbed the sleeve of her jacket. So many thoughts were going through her mind. Her encounter with the polar bear had scared her more than anything had ever scared her before.

"I don't understand," Haibu whispered. "I didn't know . . . "

Haibu suddenly realized what the polar bear was talking about: the coat she was wearing was

36

made from bearskin, and she would surely die from hypothermia without it

Much time passed while they floated aimlessly in the ocean. Haibu wanted to make plans for their next move, but Kanuux had fallen fast asleep, worn out from the epic battle. Feeling his warmth and stillness, the tiresome events took their toll, and she fell fast asleep, cuddled next to Kanuux.

DRIFTING

Minutes turned to hours, and hours turned to days and more days. The ice was very cold, and the beating rays of the sun were very, very hot. The already small slab of ice was melting by the minute. Kanuux dove for fish a few times a day and brought them back to the ice for the two of them.

Even with the abundance of fish, however, there was no fresh water. Without it, Haibu could not survive much longer. There was no sign of land in any direction. The floating ice shrunk smaller than the size of a door.

With dehydration setting in, Haibu became too weak to sit up or even speak. Still, Kanuux did not leave her side and continued to lie next to her, keeping her warm.

Out of nowhere, from the vast emptiness of the Atlantic Ocean, a huge cargo ship approached, its siren blaring. The men on board were shouting and pointing at the ice. "Man overboard, man overboard. There's a boy down there being attacked by a seal!"

The ship slowed and a rope ladder dropped down to the ice. Two men climbed down and made their way to Haibu, but Kanuux refused to let them get close. He growled and showed his teeth.

The men were determined to get Haibu on board safely. They kicked at Kanuux and yelled, "Get away from him!" As the men crept closer, Kanuux became frightened. He didn't want to leave Haibu, but he could not go with these men. With a heavy heart, Kanuux dove into the water.

As the men lifted Haibu up in a basket, she barely had the strength to open her eyes. She was hoisted past huge letters painted on the side of the ship that read *SADIEE-14*. With the last of her energy, Haibu whispered the words to herself, "Say-dee fourtee—" then drifted to sleep.

Another horn sounded and the ship started moving again. Kanuux popped his head out of the water. As the ship sailed away, Kanuux whimpered his first word: "Hiii-boooo." With those words, he dove underwater and raced after the ship. He popped his head up above the water every so often, hoping to get a glimpse of Haibu.

IN A NEW YORK MAYOK

Hearing murmurs, Haibu opened her eyes just enough to make out two blurry figures standing over her.

"Who is he?" said a woman's voice. "I've never seen an outfit quite like this one before." She touched Haibu's parka.

A man with a French accent responded. "I don't know, Ms. Phipps. A ship found him floating on a piece of ice. I'm surprised he's even alive."

"Well, we just don't have room for him here at The Barrington House Orphanage, Henrik. Hillcrest has a couple of open beds. Take him over there," Ms. Phipps said sternly.

"Don't you think the boy has been through enough for one day?" Henrik whispered. "And who knows how long he was out on that ice. Let's just put him in with Scotty. He needs rest."

"Okay, but if he steps one foot out of line, he's out."

Even though Haibu was a Mayok, she spoke and understood English, so she knew most of what was going on. However, she was still too weak to utter a single word. Haibu drifted back to sleep.

♥

THUMP!

Haibu woke up in a panic as something bounced off her nose. While she slept, she had been moved to a different room. She looked down to see something brown and lumpy rolling away on the floor. A small stone or piece of wood perhaps.

The room was pretty bare, with only a couple of beds, a lamp with a broken shade, and a trunk at the foot of the bed. It didn't feel like a home and only made Haibu miss hers even more.

Picking up a large glass of water beside her on the nightstand, Haibu gulped it down without taking a breath. The dehydration made her feel woozy and even more difficult to understand exactly where she was.

"Ouch!" Haibu said as she felt the wound on her left arm. "That nanuq got me good." A faint giggle came from behind the trunk at the foot of her bed.

"Who is there?" Haibu asked. She saw something

black and shiny sticking out from behind the trunk. A small boy with black hair popped up and threw another stone at her.

CRACK!

Another hit to the noggin. The attack resumed, but this time Haibu nearly fell out of bed trying to catch the stones as they bounced off her arms, face, and head. Before Haibu could launch a counter-attack, the boy raced over to her.

"Hi, I'm Scotty! I'm eleven. Do you like peanuts?" He poured the peanuts onto her lap. She held one up to the light, trying to figure out what it was.

Scotty asked, "What's your name? They said you was a boy. You a boy? You're so bundled up you look like the marshmallow man from *Ghostbusters*. You ever seen that movie? I like it. You like movies? I got a whole bunch under the bed if you want to watch."

There was no stopping Scotty, which was good because Haibu didn't feel like talking just yet. She just stared at him, wide-eyed.

"Hey, how old are you? Have you met Ms. Phipps? She's the mean old lady who runs this place. She smells like my gym socks. She doesn't like peanuts,

even though her head looks like a peanut."

Scotty burst out laughing while poking Haibu's arm. "Did you hear that? Did you hear that? Ha-ha-ha-ha! I said her head looks like a peanut!"

Unsure about most of Scotty's rambling, Haibu continued staring and keeping quiet. Finally he wound down and looked at Haibu with a serious expression. "Look, if we're going to be friends you're going to have to know a good joke when you hear one," he insisted. "I'm going to assume, because you're wrapped up in that coat tighter than a pig in a blanket, that maybe you didn't hear the joke. I'm going to let that one slide, because you will soon figure out that I just might be the funniest kid in New York City."

Haibu looked straight into Scotty's eyes and thought, *Did he say New York City? He couldn't . . . I mean . . . I can't possibly be in New York!* Haibu had heard tales about the great village of New York City, with houses that reached the clouds and more people than there were fish in the ocean.

She took a deep breath. "New York City?"

"Hey, he talks! Yeah, New York City. By the way,

where are you from? You talk like your mouth is full of marbles. I bet it's New Jersey, isn't it? Aw, I'm sorry about that. Some of us just have bad luck in life. Met a kid from Jersey like you once; didn't turn out so great for him."

Worried she would never be reunited with her family, Haibu crawled to the head of the bed and peered out the window. She was eight stories up in the sky. Down below she saw the bustling nighttime city. Cars plowed through slushy, snow-covered streets and people walked briskly with purpose every which way.

"Whoa," Haibu gasped.

"Whoa is right," Scotty replied. "Not the Jersey Shore, huh, bub." He rolled his eyes and muttered, "Thank goodness for that. Are you gonna eat those?" Scotty asked, pointing at the pile of peanuts.

There was an awkward pause as they stared at each other.

"Um . . . Do you need me to speak slower?" Scotty asked. He picked up a peanut and held it in the air. "This . . . is a . . . peee-nuuut. You eeeeaaat it . . . like thiiiiiiiiis—"

CRACK!

Right between the eyes! Before Scotty could finish, Haibu hit him with a flying peanut that bounced right off his forehead. Her aim was impeccable. She crossed her arms and scowled.

"Geez, you could have just marbled that to me, Jersey." Scotty cracked the peanut shell in two and sucked out one of the nuts inside. "See, bub, that's how you eat a peanut."

When he handed Haibu the other peanut, she was puzzled. "Is this food?" she asked. "It doesn't look like any food I have seen before."

While Haibu was carefully inspecting the peanut, Scotty reached over and slapped the bottom of her hand, sending it flying into the air. Like a baseball outfielder he circled under it. "I got it, I got it!" he said, then caught the peanut in his mouth. "You gotta be quicker than that, you walking furball!" Scotty laughed.

Haibu frowned, cracked open another peanut shell, and quickly gobbled both peanuts inside, so Scotty didn't get another chance to pop it out of her hand. After several days of floating on the ice with

very little food, Haibu devoured the entire pile of peanuts in a few minutes.

"Whoa, furball, you're like a machine!" Scotty teased.

There was another moment of silence, then tears rolled down Haibu's cheeks as reality began to set in. Home was far away, and Haibu had no idea where her parents were. Were they looking for her? Were they scared like her? Overwhelmed with sadness and fear, she bowed her head and cried into her hands.

Scotty tried to console her. "I didn't mean anything by it, furball. It's just that you look like you're wearing an entire bear."

This did not help. Haibu's glare shot through

Scotty as she remembered the polar bear's words. Haibu yanked at the coat, trying to pull it off.

"What did I do?" Scotty asked.

With tears flowing full force, she said, "I need a coat. I can't . . . I can't wear this anymore. Please, Scotty, a coat."

Scotty stood there, stunned. "Are you okay?"

"Please, a new coat."

"Um, I only have this one coat. I could trade you? You can wear mine and I can wear—"

"No!" Haibu yelled.

She rubbed her sleeves and said, "No one can ever wear this coat again. This coat could have been an Atata, or an Anana, or a cub. It was a living thing, like you and me. I never thought about it living, breathing, and loving before, until I met the nanuq. He was right. And this coat needs to go away, Scotty. It needs to go away forever . . . Please."

Scotty opened the trunk and rummaged around. "Here! I found something! You can wear these." He pulled out a large, blue sweatshirt with the letters NYC on it, and an old pair of jeans.

"Take them," he offered. "The sweatshirt even has a hood like yours, and I'm sure we can find you some shoes here in the house."

Haibu began to realize that Scotty was actually a good guy. In spite of all his babbling and teasing.

"Mr. Henrik said I need to keep giving you water," he reported. "I'll go fill this up and you can change. Is that cool, bub?"

Wiping away tears, Haibu gave a small smile and nodded her head. When Scotty returned with the glass of water, Haibu was sound asleep. She was neatly curled up in the oversized sweatshirt with the hood covering her head. Scotty grabbed Haibu's old coat off the floor and walked to the trash chute at the end of the hallway.

"Well, old coat, nobody will ever be wearing you again." Scotty tossed the coat down the chute and waited until he heard it hit the bottom.

OUT LIKE A LIGHT

The next morning, with her hood covering most of her face, Haibu found herself sitting at a lunch table and being stared at by Scotty and two other boys.

"I'm Ollie," one said to Haibu. "I can read minds and tell the future." He looked a little older than Scotty, and was a little chubby, with freckles and red hair.

"Not true," Scotty whispered.

The other boy looked a little older than the others, with dark hair like Scotty's, but curlier than she'd ever seen. "I'm Zeek. Who are you?" he asked.

"Wait!" Ollie jumped in. "Don't tell us. I shall tell *you*." Ollie closed his eyes and placed his fingers on his temples.

"Oh, Ollie! Just quit with this crazy stuff. You can't read minds!" Zeek exclaimed.

"Yeah, Ollie, it never works. Give it up." Scotty laughed.

Ollie ignored both of them and continued with his eyes closed. "You . . . you are from New York

City and your parents dropped you off here . . . and they told you they would be back in twenty minutes . . . and that was five years ago." He opened his eyes and looked at Haibu. "Am I right?"

Scotty shook his head and replied, "No, you're not right! He got here *yesterday* and that New York hoodie is mine."

"And just because *your* parents did that to you, Ollie, doesn't mean that's how everyone got here," Zeek said.

"Okay, okay. We're all pretty much misfits around here. So, whoever you are, welcome." Ollie said.

Haibu found herself staring at the boys, then staring at the breakfast bowls in front of them, including hers. They were packed full of white and mushy oatmeal, but not like any oatmeal Haibu had ever tasted before. The three boys were hardly touching theirs.

Haibu looked at them, then back at her bowl. It had been days since she had a real meal, and she wasn't willing to let this opportunity pass her by. Haibu grabbed the spoon and shoveled bite after bite after every little bite into her mouth. The boys were mesmerized. To their amazement, she devoured half the bowl in less than a minute!

"Slow down, you're gonna to get a bellyache eating like that," Zeek scolded.

Scotty laughed. "It's the wanna-be oatmeal that's gonna give him a bellyache."

Haibu continued to stuff her mouth.

"What's your name?" asked Ollie.

"Good luck with that, this one barely talks," Scotty said with a laugh.

Haibu kept eating.

"Hey, newbie! What's your name?" Zeek asked as he slid his bowl over to Haibu. "I'll give you mine if you tell us your name."

Haibu grabbed Zeek's bowl and shouted, "Haibu!"

Then she dug into his food as well.

"Bless you," Ollie replied.

Zeek laughed. "He didn't sneeze. That's his name. Haibu, right?"

Haibu looked up. "That's right. Haibu."

Scotty threw his hands in the air, "Haibu, boo-boo or koo-koo-ka-choo! All I know is this kid is from Jersey, so he definitely needs us to look after him."

The three boys laughed.

Haibu finished her second bowl of oatmeal and glanced around the room. She immediately felt overwhelmed. Nothing looked familiar. No faces she recognized. What had she done? She wished she had never tried to prove herself to her family.

"How could I have been so silly?" she muttered to herself, dropping her head down on the table.

The boys kept talking, but Haibu heard none of their words until Scotty leaned over and whispered in her ear, "Want to get out of here?"

Haibu raised her head and nodded and he waved for her to follow him. They headed for the door.

"Wait! You're gonna eat my food and just take off?" yelled Zeek.

Ollie pointed at Zeek, laughing, "Your oatmeal got jacked by a sneeze."

Zeek glared at Ollie and shook his head. "And if you really could read minds, you would've seen that coming."

♥

Scotty and Haibu made their way outside to the alley behind the orphanage.

"Cold, I know, but it looked like you needed some fresh air."

"Thank you," Haibu replied.

"I know you're sad and I guess you will tell me about it when you're ready, but what makes you happy?" Scotty asked.

Haibu said nothing and, again, just stared at him. Scotty urged her to tell him. "Happy? Like . . . smiles and fun things?"

Haibu looked up and down the alley and saw

people dumping trash. A few men were arguing over a fish delivery out of the back door of a restaurant. Haibu answered, "Home. Montooka."

"I don't know where that is, but we all want to go home. Problem is, if you're here, it's because you don't have a home. The faster you get comfortable with that, the better off you will be." Scotty was trying to comfort her the best way he knew how.

Thinking about Kanuux and the bear, Haibu wondered, *Can I really talk to animals? Is the nanuq the only animal that can understand me? Maybe if I can find—*

"Nanuq," blurted Haibu.

"Nanuq? What is that?" asked Scotty.

Haibu didn't know the English word, so she acted like a bear, holding her hands above her head and bending her fingers like claws. *"Roooaaar,"* Haibu growled.

"That's a nanuq?" Scotty made the same expression as Haibu and growled, "Rawr!"

Haibu jumped with excitement. "Yes! Nanuq! Nanuq!"

"That's a bear! And I know exactly where a bear

is! There is a circus not far from here. Let's go!"

Haibu yelled, "Bear! Bear! Bear!" as she ran behind Scotty, full speed toward the city streets.

THE NOT-SO-GREATEST
SHOW ON EARTH

With Scotty leading the way, the two ran for what seemed like forever. Haibu stopped halfway across the Brooklyn Bridge to catch her breath.

"Scotty . . . I have to stop," Haibu gasped, and then looked between the bars to stare at the most magnificent thing she had ever seen: the Statue of Liberty. Haibu moved closer and pushed her face between the bars of the railing.

"Scotty, what is it?'"

"Really?" Scotty asked. "That's Lady Liberty. You know, you can see her from New Jersey. Just saying."

"Who is she?" asked Haibu.

"She was a gift from France. For America becoming a country on its own and to remind us that slavery is bad."

"She's beautiful," Haibu whispered. "What is slavery?"

"Um, slavery . . . So, it's like keeping people caged and making them work for no money. Um . . .

what else? Making people do things for you and not letting them be free. Mr. Henrik said it's like controlling things with fear. I don't think anybody does it anymore," Scotty explained.

Haibu tried to understand what Scotty was saying. "Oh! Like sled dogs?" she asked.

"No, Haibu," Scotty said, with a confused look on his face. "Slavery is for *people* held against their will."

Haibu thought back to how they kept dogs pinned up in Montooka and made them pull their sleds in the deep of winter.

"So, like sled dogs," Haibu stated emphatically. "We keep them in a pen and then we make them pull our sleds. They don't eat unless we feed them and they don't have free time unless we allow them."

Scotty replied, "Dogs are not people, Haibu. Slavery is for people."

"So, slavery is bad? It makes people sad?" Haibu asked.

"Well, yes. It's bad because it makes them sad."

"Then why not for dogs? Don't dogs get sad too?"

"Well, I guess so, but it's different. It's people."

Haibu peered back over the bridge to get one last

glimpse of the Statue of Liberty. "Like sled dogs," she whispered to herself.

"We should go, Haibu," Scotty urged. "The circus is in Brooklyn, and we need to be back at The Barrington House before dinner. If we aren't on time Ms. Phipps goes *minnow paws*."

"What's *minnow paws*?" Haibu asked.

"It's what Mr. Henrik says happens to Ms. Phipps when she gets angry for no reason. Not sure what she has against fish feet, but I don't want to see her mad about it."

Scotty and Haibu continued across the Brooklyn Bridge. Haibu was in awe of the view. Below the statue there were many boats in the water and helicopters in the blue sky. Haibu was actually enjoying herself for the first time since becoming lost.

As they left the bridge, Scotty called out "Welcome to Brooklyn!" and they ran through streets lined with warehouses and shipping containers. Haibu saw a big sign that read "Brooklyn Yard Circus" and heard the faint sound of music in the distance.

"Almost there!" Scotty yelled. "Follow me!" He ducked into an alleyway behind a warehouse.

Haibu followed Scotty to a maintenance entrance located at the back of the building, near the water. The music was loud and the circus ringmaster could be heard over the megaphone. "That's right, ladies, gentlemen, and children of all ages."

Scotty and Haibu crawled under the grandstand bleachers and started watching the show. Scotty grabbed a small paper bag from a bench next to someone's foot. "Want some?" he offered.

"What is it?" Haibu asked.

"Popcorn. It's a vegetable."

Haibu took a piece of popcorn loaded with butter and salt and popped it into her mouth.

"You like it?" Scotty asked.

"I don't know, but I think it's stuck." Haibu pointed to her throat.

"Hold on," Scotty instructed.

Scotty then slid down a bit and grabbed a soda sitting on the bench. "Here, wash it down with this."

Haibu washed down the popcorn with the soda and winced as it burned her throat. Her attention was back on the circus ringmaster as he continued spoke through the microphone. "Who dares brave the ring of terror with these vicious lions, tigers, and bears?"

Haibu got excited. "Bears, Scotty! He said bears!"

"Shhh!" Scotty put his hand over Haibu's mouth. "Quiet. This isn't New Jersey. We have to be quiet during the show."

Haibu nodded. When the lights came on full blast, Haibu saw strange-looking people she'd never seen before. They had wild curly hair, big red noses, and giant feet. And there were a bunch of identical but tiny ones chasing after them.

"What are those?" Haibu whispered to Scotty.

"Clowns. They make people laugh."

Haibu pointed at the long line of little clowns following the big one. "They have lots of young."

Scotty giggled, "Those aren't babies, those are little people. Little grown-up people."

"They stay little forever?"

"Yeah, they're just like big people, except they just stay, well, they just stay little."

"Sometimes I think want to stay little," Haibu whispered.

Scotty pointed to his head. "I thought I did too, but think about always having to climb for the cookie jar. Huh, see what I'm saying? I'm a genius."

BOOM!

Loud explosions lit up the room as the main event began. Sitting in the middle of the ring was a tiger, a lion, and a large elephant, all standing on stools with heavy chains around their necks. With a whip in one hand, the announcer continued, "I will brave these ferocious beasts and put my life on the line for your enjoyment!"

Haibu watched in silence, barely blinking. She did not understand what was going on or what kind of show this was. She had just battled a polar bear in the wild and this man was calling himself brave with three chained animals in front of him. Haibu understood the word "brave," as it was often used in her village.

Haibu leaned over toward Scotty. "He wouldn't know brave if it bit him on his rear."

Scotty covered his mouth as he and Haibu giggled wildly.

CRACK!

They are both startled by the sound. The ringmaster had cracked his whip at the lion.

CRACK!

The ringmaster whipped the lion again and pointed to the floor, making him follow instructions.

CRACK! CRACK!

The lion winced and roared in pain.

Haibu covered her mouth with her hand. Everyone in the bleachers, young and old, cheered and clapped. Haibu turned to Scotty and motioned to the little kids near them. "Why are they happy? This is horrible. These animals are hurting! Why would that man whip them?"

With each crack of the whip, Haibu winced.

Again and again.

"You've never been to a circus before?" Scotty asked.

"No." Haibu shuddered.

"Let's get out of here." He grabbed Haibu's hand and pulled her back out the maintenance doors.

♥

As they stepped out into the alleyway, Haibu turned and looked back at the circus.

"This was a bad idea," Scotty said. "I'm sorry. Let's just get back to The Barrington House."

"I can't leave yet. I need to talk to them!" Haibu explained.

"To who?"

"To the animals, Scotty. I need to speak to them about getting home."

Scotty stared at his feet, placed his hands on his head and exhaled deeply. "This is getting looney."

"I'm not looney, Scotty!" Haibu yelled. "I need to talk to those animals!"

"Look, Haibu, you're saying you can talk to animals. You know what they do to kids who say stuff like that at The Barrington House? They lock them away upstate in what's called the peanut house. I heard all about it! This one kid, Marcus—"

"Stop it, Scotty! I'm not going to the peanut house! I need to see if those animals can talk so I can try and get home. I don't live at The Barrington House, and I'm not from Jersey! I live in Montooka!"

Haibu stomped back toward the circus.

For a moment, Scotty thought about heading home on his own. Then he shrugged and followed behind her, muttering to himself, "You're going to wish you lived at The Barrington House when they lock you up with the peanuts."

LIONS, TIGERS, AND BEARS, OH LIE!

They waited a little while until the afternoon show ended. Men from the circus forced the animals back into their cages. A horn blew, calling the workers to dinner.

"The horn means we have about an hour until the evening show," Scotty explained. "Make it quick, Haibu!"

Haibu and Scotty snuck around to the opposite side of the trailers, where each animal could be seen through its cage. The first cage was full of chimpanzees. Haibu had only seen monkeys in pictures from books the elders passed down. This was her first time seeing these animals in real life.

The chimpanzees' heads hung low, barely acknowledging either of the children. Haibu approached one that was closest to the bars.

"Hi, I'm Haibu. What is your name?"

The chimpanzee didn't acknowledge her. He just sat quietly, staring at the floor, running one finger through the straw. No expression, just a blank stare.

"Are they tired?" Haibu asked Scotty.

"They look sad," Scotty answered. "I've never seen a monkey so sad, much less a group of them."

"Monkeys?" Haibu asked.

"Yeah, they're called monkeys, chimps, apes, whatever. They should be swinging, screaming, and throwing poo at you."

"Scotty, no!" Haibu exclaimed.

"Hey—monkey see, monkey doo-doo," Scotty giggled.

Haibu shook her head, then turned back to the chimp. "Can you understand me?"

"Come on, Haibu. We're already late for dinner!" Scotty grabbed Haibu's arm, but she was not ready to go. She pulled away and turned back to the cage.

"Please, Mr. Monkey, please! I need you to answer me!"

Still nothing. The chimpanzee didn't even lift his head in Haibu's direction. Haibu dropped to her knees on the straw-covered pavement. She covered her eyes with her hands and began to cry.

"Where am I?" she whispered, more to herself

than the monkey. "Where are my parents? Where are you guys? Come find me, please!"

Scotty stood, paralyzed. "Come on, Haibu, I'm sorry. It's just a stupid ole monkey anyhow. He ain't no good for nothing." Scotty put his hand on Haibu's shoulder. "Haibu, really, we have to leave."

Haibu continued to cry, holding her head in her hands. Her emotions from the confusion of not knowing where she was, or how she got there, got the best of her. She had all but given up.

"He's not a stupid monkey," said a very deep, calm voice.

Haibu turned around, but no one was there. She looked back at the chimp.

"Did you say something?" Haibu asked, gripping the bars of the cage with every ounce of her strength.

The same voice replied, "It was me."

As Haibu looked for its source, Scotty asked her, "Who are you talking to?"

"Quiet, Scotty," Haibu replied.

The voice spoke again. "Two trailers down. Come."

Haibu moved toward the source of the voice. Scotty followed.

"Haibu?" he asked.

"Someone is talking—follow me!" answered Haibu.

As they turned the corner, they saw a cage and inside was the lion from the main event. He was pacing back and forth.

"Was that you? Can you talk?" Haibu asked the lion.

"He's not a stupid monkey," the lion shot back.

"I'm sorry, he didn't mean that." Haibu turned to Scotty pleading, "Tell him you didn't mean that."

Scotty was confused. "Tell who? That growling lion?"

Haibu said, "Yes! Tell him."

"Haibu, we really need to go," Scotty said.

"He can't understand me," said the lion.

"Why not?"

"Because he is human."

"But aren't I human, too?"

The lion stopped pacing and looked Haibu in the eyes. "That is the real question at hand, isn't it?"

Haibu was confused. "I don't understand. Why can't he hear you like I can?"

"Because he only chooses to see the world as it is

presented to him and fails to look deeper."

Haibu looked back at Scotty, who shrugged his shoulders. He only saw and heard a lion growling back at her. "I don't understand. Why can't he hear you?"

"He has not learned that every living thing is alive, with feelings, and should be treated as such!"

"I've done all of that?" Haibu asked.

"You must have, little Haibu. Here you stand, speaking with the animals."

"Tell me more. What is your name? How am I able to talk to some animals?"

The lion leaned toward her. "My name is Eron. If you really want to know the answer to that question, pay close attention to what I am about to tell you. Every single living organism, at one point in time, could communicate with one another. We worked together to grow and become living creatures, like you and those you see around you. At some point in history, humans created their own *so-called* 'laws of society.' "

Eron resumed pacing back and forth as he spoke. "Those laws made the humans feel like they were no longer sharing the earth with animals, but instead were the masters of all living beings. Before man developed his own language, he was much more in tune with other living creatures, even the plants that supply him oxygen. We could all speak and understand one another!"

Eron raised his voice and made a fist with his right paw. "The desire to be different without accepting differences in others is, and will ultimately be, mankind's downfall. Once they divided their beliefs and nationalities, they no longer saw even each other as equals, only as different. Unfortunately for the animals, we were the first to be taken advantage of. Once man had a grasp on us, they turned their attention on each other. They enslaved and oppressed those who dared to be different. Man is too consumed with the ideal that they need to be the biggest, the best, and the wealthiest, when they should be striving to be the most honest and compassionate."

"Why did humans do this?" asked Haibu.

"No one knows," Eron replied sadly. "Greed, gluttony, and a lack of love, empathy, and compassion have consumed the earth. All living beings are no longer treated as equal."

Scotty walked over to Haibu. "Look, bub, you've had enough time. This lion isn't going to talk."

"Why does he call you 'bub'?" the lion asked.

"He thinks I'm a boy," she answered, then turned to Scotty. "By the way, I'm not a boy. And my name is Haibu, not 'bub.'" Haibu pulled the hood off her head, revealing her long, flowing hair, with some strands sporting beads like those of the Shookia.

Scotty's eyes grew as big as baseballs.

"Wait . . . you . . . boy . . . Jersey?" Scotty looked stunned as he plopped down on the ground.

Eron and Haibu stared at Scotty for a moment, then Haibu broke the silence. "So, what about food? I've eaten more animals than I want to remember," she admitted.

"Hunting to survive is nature. Hunting for fun is lunacy," Eron replied.

Haibu thought for a moment. "Do you know what I need to do to get home?" she asked.

"You're asking the wrong question, little girl," said a new voice.

"Who said that?" Looking into the trailer on her left, Haibu saw a very large elephant that was hunching down so it could fit inside its small cage.

"That's Wiz," Eron said. "He might be too wise for his own good."

"Oh, you poor soul, you can't even fit in there. How long have they kept you locked up like this?"

"Twenty-two years," answered the elephant.

Haibu stepped backward with her hand on her heart. "That's more than twice as old as I am. I'm so sorry."

"What were you getting at, Wiz?" asked Eron, "The child only has a few minutes before the workers return."

"I said the girl was asking the wrong question." Wiz turned toward Haibu. "You need to find out what your purpose is, little girl. You do that, and home will find you."

Eron chuckled. "Home will find you. Wiz, that small cage is starting to make you crazy." Eron continued his pacing, muttering and laughing to himself. "Home will find you, pffft!"

Wiz turned back to Haibu. "Haibu, is it?" he asked.

"Yes, it is."

"What I'm saying is that you obviously have a higher purpose than just returning home. I assume you are from the north?"

"Why, yes. Montooka! How did you know? Do you know where it is?" Haibu asked.

"It's your eyes, my little Haibu, the eyes. I do not know of Montooka."

"I need to get back ther—"

"Do you?" Wiz interrupted.

"Of course she does, Wiz. It's the child's home. She's lost!" Eron replied.

"Pipe down!" Wiz cried. "This is no ordinary child and she isn't standing here by chance! The universe must have set this in motion!"

"What do you mean? Why am I here?" Haibu asked.

"The universe sent you, Haibu."

Eron jumped to the side of the cage closest to Wiz. "You cannot put this responsibility on a child. It is too dangerous!"

"This child is one of the chosen! She is not even of this land and yet she stands before us. Allow her to make her own decision."

"She could be killed!" Eron growled.

Wiz poked his trunk out of the cage at Haibu. "Haibu, you need to make this dangerous decision on your own. You have a purpose and when you realize what that is and act on it, *home . . . will . . . find . . . you.*"

Haibu looked at Scotty and then back to Wiz. "So if I help you animals, I will go home? Is that what you're saying?"

The sound of a metal door slamming echoed through the cages and brought the conversation to a halt.

"Hey! You kids get out of here! Scram, you varmints!" A circus worker was running toward Haibu and Scotty.

Scotty leaped up, grabbed Haibu's hand, and pulled her away. "We have to go! Now!"

Eron yelled, "Run, Haibu! Run!"

The man reached the cage and heard the lion growling. He took out a whip and cracked it through the bars, squarely across Eron's back. Eron wailed in pain.

Looking back as she ran, Haibu screamed, "No! Leave him alone!"

"You come back again, you little brat, and I'll give you the same!" yelled the man.

Scotty and Haibu ran until the circus disappeared behind them.

♥

Back at the cages, Wiz whispered to Eron, "She is one of the chosen, Eron. She can do incredible things if she sets her mind to it."

Eron replied, "You're an old fool, Wiz. We will never see that child again."

"We aren't the only animals in captivity. If not us, she will help others."

RALLY THE TROOPS

Later that evening, Scotty and Haibu were sitting in their room at The Barrington House when there was a knock at the door.

"That must be them," Scotty announced.

He opened the door, letting in Zeek and Ollie. Scotty peered out and checked each end of the hallway before closing the door. The coast was clear; on with the meeting.

"This better be good. I was about to watch a movie," Zeek said as he walked in.

Scotty said, "Everyone, sit down."

"Uh oh, this must be important," said Ollie.

Scotty motioned for Haibu to stand beside him. "Guys, this is Haibu."

"Um, Scotty, we know this already. He ate my food, remember?" Zeek said.

"No, guys, *this* is Haibu!" Scotty pulled off Haibu's hood, revealing her long hair.

Stunned, Zeek blurted out, "Oh snap, dude look like a lady!"

"Dude *is* a lady," Scotty replied.

"I'm Haibu and I'm a girl," Haibu announced firmly. "And we need your help!"

"What happened? Do we need to find someone? Because I could use my powers and find someone with a quickness!" Ollie held his hand in the air to high-five Zeek.

Zeek stared at Ollie, shaking his head. "Just quit, dude."

"Guys, pay attention, please!" Scotty shouted. "You see, Haibu here can talk to animals."

Ollie and Zeek's mouths dropped open. They slowly turned to each other and then burst out laughing.

"Ha-ha-ha! Did you just hear that?" Ollie cackled.

Zeek wiped tears from his eyes. "Man, Scotty, you're a fool, but I love you man."

"Guys, I'm serious, we went to the circus and she was having a conversation with them."

Zeek and Ollie listened intently. "You heard the animals talk too, Scotty?" asked Ollie.

"No, but I know what a conversation looks like. Animal or human!"

Both Zeek and Ollie started rolling around, laughing and slapping the floor.

"He's telling the TRUTH!" Haibu screamed.

Both boys stopped rolling around and pulled themselves together. They could see that Haibu wasn't in a joking mood.

"Have you two ever been to a circus?" Haibu asked.

"Yes, of course we have," said Ollie.

"Well, then you should both know the terrible things that are happening to those animals."

The boys shrugged their shoulders. "Scotty, what is she talking about?" Zeek asked.

Scotty explained, "Guys you know all the tricks the animals do, right? Jump from chair to chair. Ride a bike—"

"Yeah, and jump through a ring of fire!" Ollie added.

"Yes. Exactly. They jump through a ring of fire. Now, how do they get them to do that?" Scotty asked.

"They crack a whip!" Zeek shouted.

"Correct again. So think about it," Scotty continued. "They crack a whip every time they want an animal to do a trick. Are you following what I'm saying?"

Ollie replied, "I don't know what the big deal is."

After a few seconds of silence, there was a *WHAP!* Haibu slapped Ollie across his forearm with a belt she grabbed off the bed.

"Ow—that hurt! What's the big idea, Haibu?"

"Imagine that happening to you a hundred times a day!" Haibu asserted. "So some kid can cheer while eating fluffy vegetable food that gets stuck in his throat."

"She's talking about popcorn," Scotty explained.

Zeek nodded. "Oh yeah, I hate when it scratches your—"

"Guys, please!" Haibu interrupted. "I talked to them today. These animals are hurting. They need our help. It will also help me get home."

Ollie looked confused. "Jersey is right over there if you just take the L—"

Scotty kicked Ollie.

"Everyone needs to stop hitting me!"

"She's not from Jersey! She's from somewhere up north, probably some new borough in Queens.

Wherever it is, I couldn't find it on the Internet. But I know she's telling the truth. We have to help these animals get out of the circus. Are you guys in or out?" Scotty asked.

Zeek thought about it. "We could get into trouble."

"Really? Trouble?" asked Scotty. "We live in an orphanage! What more could possibly happen to us?"

Zeek and Ollie looked at each other, then shouted, "We're in!"

"Great!" said Haibu. "Here's the plan . . ."

PRE-GAME

It had been a full day since they put their plan into action. The four of them sat huddled on the floor with newspapers and phone books scattered all around them. Ollie was on a call with one of the trucking companies.

". . . I mean, yes, that's what I'm asking you," Ollie said.

The man on the speakerphone was from the transportation company and sounded very confused. "So, let me get this straight, you need two semi-trucks—"

"That's right," replied Ollie.

"And you need them to move animals from Red Hook Channel to Sunny View Animal Sanctuary in Hartford?

"Yep!"

"Who are you, Noah?" asked the man.

"No, I'm Ollie! Who is Noah?"

"Like the ark."

"What's an ark?"

"It's a boat . . . a boat that carries animals. Noah's Ark?" the man asks.

"Hold on." Ollie covered the speaker and looked at the other kids. "Did you know about this guy named Noah who has a boat to carry animals? I say we just call him."

Zeek lifted Ollie's hand off the speaker and said to the man on the phone. "Sir, we will have to call you back!" He hung up the phone. "Ollie, you nitwit! That's Noah's Ark, the Bible story!" Zeek said.

"Well, fine then, if you guys don't like the way I'm doing it, you can do this yourself! And another thing, I'm going to wear a president's mask during this heist, whether you like it or not!" Ollie shouted.

"It's not a heist—it's an animal rescue!" Scotty yelled back. "And for all I care, you can wear a pink tutu. Just stay focused!"

A quick knock on the door made everyone freeze. They held their breaths as the door slowly opened.

"Hey kids," Henrik whispered as he stuck his head in the doorway. The kids let out sighs of relief that it wasn't Ms. Phipps.

"Hey Mr. Henrik. We were just, uh, just making

prank phone calls!" blurted Ollie.

"Wow, Ollie," Scotty said, "Is that the best you could come up with?"

"You know anyone who picks up another phone in this house can hear your call, right?" Henrik asked.

No one answered.

"Just keep the noise to a minimum. Goodnight, kids," Henrik said with a wink before leaving.

Zeek stood up. "I am *not* getting my dessert privileges taken away for this."

Scotty yanked him back to the floor and continued flipping through the phone book. "Zeek, focus. What is the name of another animal rescue company?"

"Ugh. Fine. Here's one called Baby Joey's Animal Rescue," Zeek replied.

"Guys, maybe we should find another rescue company to call. I feel like *Baby Joey* sounds like we're trying to raise money for some poor kid's heart transplant," stated Ollie.

Scotty was confused. "What? Ollie, what are you even saying right now? It's a rescue company, and we obviously can't let you make any more calls. So, no, we will call this one too!"

"*Okayyyyy, but all I'm saying iiiiissss* . . . If some poor kid named Joey ever gets sick, he'll never be able to raise money on the Internet because we are supporting the company that stole his name. That's all I'm saying," Ollie explained.

Zeek shook his head in disbelief. "I often wonder how you made it this far in life."

Haibu stood to stretch a bit. She walked over and peered through the darkness toward the partially lit wharf across the street. There were huge barges lined in a row, larger than some of the villages near Montooka. She saw bits of water between them and decided to get some air by taking a walk near the vessels. She was feeling nervous and thought the water might calm her down, remind her of home.

"I'm going for a quick walk," announced Haibu.

"Wait, Haibu, nighttime in New York isn't the best place for little kids. I'll come with you," Scotty offered.

"No, I'll be fine," Haibu replied. "I want to be alone for a few minutes. Please." Haibu snuck down the stairs and headed out across the snow-covered streets toward the wharf.

Lost in thought as she walked along the docks, Haibu tried to make sense of everything that she learned in the past few days. *I don't know what to do. How do I get home? Why isn't my family looking for me?* So many thoughts were racing through Haibu's mind. She looked up to the sky for answers.

"Please, if anyone can hear me—" Something caught Haibu's eye. "Sadiee dash one four," she muttered, as her eyes moved across the front of a ship. "Sadiee dash one four!" she screamed. "Sadiee dash fourteen! That's it! That's the boat! That's my BOAT!" Haibu jumped up and down and screamed at the top of her lungs, "SADIEE DASH FOURTEEN!"

Haibu's celebration was short-lived, however. She suddenly realized that just because this boat picked her up from a piece of floating ice didn't mean the crew knew where Montooka was. Haibu sat down on the pier and dangled her feet over the ocean. In the waters below, she imagined a faint image of her father and brother heading out on their fishing expedition. The movement of the water scrambled the image, and then she could see her mother cooking in the kitchen, just as she was when Haibu last saw her.

"I miss you guys," Haibu whispered.

Another faint image appeared in the water; it was Kanuuk. Haibu cracked a smile. She could see his little face getting bigger by the second.

"Wait. Is that—"

SPLASH!

Suddenly, Kanuux leaped from the ocean, right into Haibu's lap. Soaking wet and cold, Haibu was showered with kisses from Kanuux.

"Kanuux! I can't believe you're here! How did you find me? Do you know where home is?"

Kanuux pulled away and looked at Haibu with his head tilted to the side, as if trying to understand. "Home, Kanuux. Where you found me—do you know where that is?"

"Haibuuuuuu," Kanuux stuttered.

"Yes! Yes!" Haibu hugged Kanuux, "You can speak! Do you know where home is?"

"Haibuuuuuu," Kanuux said again as he licked her face.

Even though she didn't understand much about how her animal communication worked, Haibu guessed that Kanuux's vocabulary must still be very small.

"Kanuux, you must have followed the boat all the way here! And you've been waiting for me this

whole time!"

Still licking Haibu's face, Kanuux made her giggle. "Well, thank you. I won't ever let us get separated again!" Haibu hugged Kanuux tighter. She didn't want to let go.

"Haibuuuuuu!" Kanuux called.

Haibu spent nearly an hour cuddling with Kanuux, telling him all about the circus and everything else she had seen. Kanuux made her feel at peace and reminded her of home. She told Kanuux to wait for her to return. She had one more animal to speak with that night. Kanuux watched as Haibu scurried towards the Brooklyn Bridge.

THE PLANIMALS

The big day finally arrived. It had been five full days since Haibu and Scotty visited the circus, and now the plan was being put in motion.

In the alley, Scotty, Zeek, and Ollie went over the details one last time as they waited for Haibu to emerge from The Barrington House. Scotty was dressed as a clown, and both Ollie and Zeek were wearing delivery outfits and holding clipboards.

Scotty was as serious as either of the other boys had ever seen him. "Okay, guys, we have to get this right. Ollie, you're in Truck One with Sid the delivery driver. Zeek, you're in Truck Two with whatever that guy's name is. Zeek, you're sure the drivers understand what we're doing? They're good with this?"

"I gave them the money that Mr. Henrik loaned us and said don't ask no questions and do as you're told," Zeek replied.

"And that worked?" Scotty asked.

"Honestly, they really didn't care once we gave

them the cash," Zeek answered.

"Okay then. We have a mission to complete, let's not forget that. These animals need us!" Scotty shouted.

Both Zeek and Ollie nodded in agreement. Scotty continued, "Once Haibu and I sneak into the arena, we will fall in line with the other clowns as they march around the main ring of the circus. We'll blend in so we can get the key hanging on the ringmaster's belt. That's the only way for us to unlock the cages."

Scotty showed them a hand-drawn map of the area. "Once we get the keys, we will run out of the maintenance door in the back of the building and give you the signal. Ollie, you need to have your driver reverse the truck so it's close enough to the building to block the door. No one can get out that back door! Once we load up Truck One, we will tell the circus workers inside that the animals out back are missing. When they run out to check on them, we will take the animals from the main show out the front door into Truck Two with you, Zeek."

Ollie stared down at the ground.

"Ollie," Scotty grabbed his arm. "Are you with us?"

Ollie looked up, nervously. "Yeah, I'm with you. I just—"

"You just, what?" Zeek asked. "We've been working on this for days; you can't wimp out on us now!"

"I'm not wimping out! Look, guys, have any of you stopped to think that we are opening the cages of wild animals and rescuing them from circus workers?" Ollie pleaded his case. "Think about it! Wild animals with teeth and claws! And circus workers! We're not talking about guys who leave the toilet seat up and don't care about the consequences. We're talking about sleeveless shirts kinda guys, who have tattoos of a heart with the word 'mom' in the middle of it! They could pummel us! We could be *that Joey kid* asking for donations to replace our broken noses!"

"Are you backing out?" Scotty asked.

"No! I just wanted to give us an alternative to possibly becoming the next picture on the back of a milk carton. That's all." Ollie pulled out a signed piece of paper that had the New York State seal printed on it.

"What is that?" Zeek asked.

"It's a letter from the governor demanding that the circus animals get released to us immediately."

Zeek snatched the letter out of Ollie's hand and read it out loud. "I hereby demand that all of the circus animals be let go to Mr. Ollie Proctor and his friends immediately! If not, I will send in the Army and a bunch of other tattooed guys."

Zeek looked up. "It's signed by Governor Walker! It has a state seal and everything! Scotty, this could work! Good job, Ollie!"

Still adjusting his clown outfit, Scotty barely paid attention after the first few words.

"So, what do you think, Scotty?" Ollie asked.

"I think you're terrible at math, Ollie."

"What?" Ollie asked, confused.

Scotty grabbed the letter and flipped it over. The other side was printed with Ollie's math homework from school. "And so will the circus workers when they see that and beat you to a pulp!"

Zeek grabbed his clipboard and bonked Ollie on top of the head with it. "I'm sorry, the computer room was out of paper and it's all I had—"

The alley door opened and out walked Haibu in her clown costume. She slid over to the boys. "Thanks again for helping me rescue these animals. And for helping me get home."

"Of course," Zeek replied.

"Did you speak to Wiz again?" Scotty asked.

"I did. I needed to understand more, so I went back again last night and spoke to him. We're doing a good thing here," Haibu replied.

Scotty took Haibu by the hand and pulled her

away from the other boys. "Haibu, I want to thank you for helping me."

"How did I help you?" Haibu asked.

"I never really had much purpose in my life so far, other than being a nuisance to the caretakers at The Barrington House. I feel like you have changed that by opening my eyes to the suffering of these poor animals. They don't have a voice, and I now realize it's so important that they do. So, thank you."

Scotty reached into his bag and pulled out a Statue of Liberty foam crown. "For you."

"Scotty, this is just like Lady Liberty's hat!"

"It is. It's a crown, and you deserve it," he said, putting the crown on her head. "You're like a real-life Lady Liberty. You're the Liberator of Animals! Let's get these animals to Sunny View so they can be

happy and have freedom to roam and play."

Haibu gave Scotty a great big bear hug that made him turn red from blushing. "You're the best, Scotty!"

The moment was interrupted by Ollie. "Hey, it's almost an hour before the first show! We need to get going! I'm never one to delay the pounding of carny fists and wild animals claws on my head! So, chop chop!"

LITTLE BIG TOPPLE

Promptly at two o'clock, music started blaring from the circus warehouse. Scotty and Haibu walked into the maintenance entrance as planned and crawled under the bleachers, where they lay in wait for the clowns to start their act.

The ringmaster stepped into the ring to start his show. "Ladies, gentlemen, and children of all ages! Are you brave enough to be in the same room with such ferocious beasts?"

Haibu saw Eron and Wiz in the center ring standing on pedestals. She nudged Scotty. "Look! There they are!"

The announcer continued, "You need not worry! I am brave enough to show these beasts who is boss!" The music in the arena was pumped up loud for the clowns as they rushed into the ring. The large clown led the group of six little clowns bobbing up and down behind him.

"This is it, Haibu! Let's go!" Scotty and Haibu scurried out from under the bleachers, then ran out

onto the circus floor—right in line with all the other little clowns. Without warning, the large clown at the front fell backward, knocking down all of the other clowns like dominos. It was part of the act, so Scotty fell as well. Haibu had no idea what was going on.

"Scotty, get up!" she shouted over the music.

"Haibu, fall!" Scotty shouted back.

"Scotty, get up! We have to get the keys!"

Scotty grabbed Haibu and yanked her down to the ground. "Fall! It's part of the act! You have to do what they do!"

"Scotty, this is dumb. They could have just moved when he fell backward. The little ones aren't very smart," Haibu said.

The clowns jumped back to their feet and circled the main ring. As they ran around, Haibu tried to get her friends' attention. "Eron! Wiz! It's me, Haibu!

Eron squinted in her direction.

CRACK!

A whip hit Eron and he roared in pain.

"Stop it!" Haibu yelled at the ringmaster. The ringmaster, confused, stared at Haibu as she ran by.

Scotty slowed down enough to pull Haibu next to him. "Keep running. And stop screaming. Do you want to get us caught?"

"No! But I want to take that whip to the announcer!"

"I get it," Scotty said. "But you have to stick to the plan."

When the music stopped, so did the big clown. All of the little clowns ran into him, falling to the floor. All except Haibu.

Haibu shouted, "Oh come on, you guys saw him stop!" She did not understand the humor of clowns.

One of the little clowns rolled over to Haibu and asked in a deep voice, "Who are you?"

"She's new!" Scotty answered as they started running again.

"And who are you?" the little clown asked.

"I'm new too!" Scotty yelled back.

Scotty turned back to Haibu. "We need to make a break for those keys NOW. Next time we pass the ringmaster, run right into him. I'll do the same and grab the keys!"

As the line of clowns passed the animals again,

Haibu yelled, "Wiz, I'm here! I've come back for you!"

Elephants have excellent hearing, so Wiz heard Haibu's voice under all the other noise. He looked down at Haibu as she ran by, and even though her face was covered in white paint and her nose was covered with a big red ball, he could still see her amazing eyes.

After years of captivity, little food, and the constant pain of being whipped, Wiz felt hope rush through him. He pulled his entire five-ton body off the ground and shouted for joy. "She's back! She's back, Eron! Little Haibu is back!"

CRACK!

The whip came down hard, smacking Wiz's trunk!

"Down!" the ringmaster shouted. "Down, you filthy beast!"

Haibu lowered her head and crashed into the ringmaster's stomach, knocking him to the ground. As planned, Scotty fell on top of him. As quickly as they fell, they were up again and sprinting away. The ringmaster clambered to his feet, dusting himself off. "Watch it, you twits, or I'll fire you both!"

The show continued as Scotty and Haibu made their way out the back door. So far, so good.

♥

Once outside, Scotty gave the signal to Ollie, who then signaled the driver. The driver reversed until the side of the truck was blocking the back door, as planned.

Ollie hopped out of the truck and ran to meet them.

"You got the keys?" Ollie asked.

"Yep!" Scotty replied.

"Anyone see you?"

"Not sure," Scotty replied. "How about we don't stick around to find out?"

"Sounds good to me!" Ollie called back as he swung open the trailer doors.

Scotty and Haibu ran to the animal cages. Scotty searched for the key that fit the lock on the chimpanzee cage.

"How did you get the keys off of him so fast?" Haibu asked.

"It's called *orphan skills*. I'll explain another time." Scotty unlocked the chimps' cage and lowered the gate. "Got it!"

"Go! Go!" Scotty yelled, but the chimpanzees were frozen, too scared to move.

"What's taking so long? They've already started printing my milk carton. Let's go!" Ollie yelled from the truck.

Scotty motioned to the chimps. "Haibu, what's wrong with them?"

Haibu reached out to one of the chimpanzees. "If you can understand me, please come with us. We are here to help you. We came back for Eron and Wiz and we will take all of you, if you let us. We will take you someplace where you will be happy and free to roam—just trust me."

The chimpanzees looked at each other.

"Scotty, stop monkeying around!" Ollie yelled.

"Put a sock in it, Ollie!"

"Please, trust us," Haibu said softly.

The chimpanzee reached out and took Haibu's hand. "That's right. Come on to the truck," Haibu coaxed. Eventually, she led all seven of the chimpanzees to the back of the trailer, hand in hand.

"Scotty, get the horses so Ollie can get them out of here," Haibu ordered.

"I'm on it!" yelled Scotty. After trying several keys, he finally unlocked the gate and the four horses followed him onto the ramp of the trailer. "Well, that's it! They're all yours, Ollie!"

Ollie slid the ramp under the trailer and locked the doors with the animals inside. "Thank you, thank you, thank you!" He sprinted to the cab of the truck and jumped in, then shouted out the window. "We did a good thing here! I really believe it."

Scotty glanced over to Haibu as she watched the truck pull away. "Whoa, is that a smile I see?"

"It is. Thank you."

Scotty reached out to squeeze Haibu's hand. "You're welcome, Haibu. Now it's time to get the others. You ready?"

"I'm ready."

"Let's do this."

Scotty ran back into the back door of the building while Haibu ran around the front to meet Zeek.

♥

"I saw the truck leave! Was it full of animals?" Zeek asked.

"It was! Just like we planned!" Haibu squeezed Zeek tight with a big hug.

Zeek yelled with excitement, "*Woohoo!* That's what *I'm* talking about!"

"You ready?" Haibu asked.

"I'm ready!" Zeek shouted.

♥

Inside the circus, no one noticed that the animals

outside were gone. Scotty told every employee he passed, "Hey, something happened to the animals and the boss needs everyone out back. Pronto!" As circus workers raced out the back door, Scotty grinned from ear to ear. His plan was working flawlessly! "I think that's all of them except the ringmaster."

Once he saw Haibu walk through the front door, he whispered to himself, "This is it."

Scotty sprinted toward the ringmaster, who was announcing the next act. "Yes, you heard me right, ladies and gents! These bears will be riding bicycles!"

Standing in the shadows, Haibu watched the show and her anger began to boil. She waited for the signal from Scotty, but it took all of her strength not to confront the circus ringmaster herself.

Seconds later, Scotty was smack in front of the ringmaster, tugging on his arm. "What?" the ringmaster yelled. "Get away from me! We're in the middle of a show! Who are you? Get out of here!"

"All of your animals are gone!"

"Scram, kid!" the ringmaster yelled. "The animals are right here!"

Scotty pointed to the maintenance entrance. "Out back! Horses and monkeys! They're gone! You need to go!"

"Kid, if you're lying, so help me you will get the wrong end of this whip!"

"Go see for yourself!"

"All right, folks, just, uh . . . keep your eyes on those bears. I'll be right back." The announcer dropped the microphone to the ground and rushed out the back door.

Haibu raced over to the lion. "Eron, it's me, Haibu!"

"Haibu? Is that really you?" Eron asked.

"Yes, I'm dressed like a clown. Hurry, you have to follow me!"

"But where are we going?"

"There's no time to talk, just follow me!"

The crowd gasped as they watched the lion and a little clown run toward the front door.

Zeek swung open the door and yelled, "Animal taxi at your service!" When he saw the lion charging straight at him, he closed his eyes and squealed, "Oh god, please! I've never done nothing to nobody.

Please don't let this lion eat me!"

Eron brushed Zeek with his fluffy mane as he rushed by him and leaped into the back of the truck. "Oh, thank you, lord!" Zeek shouted.

Haibu started to head back in. "I have to get Wiz!"

Eron yelled to her, "Bring the bears, Haibu!"

Haibu stopped in her tracks. She hadn't thought about the bears. She paused to think it out. *I have to free the nanuqs too?* She remembered again that bears in the north were not very friendly to Mayoks.

She was nervous, but her courage was there. *I can do anything I believe I can do. I can be anything I believe I can be. I can achieve anything I want to achieve. I am Haibu.*

"I can do this!" Haibu cried. "They deserve to be free too!" She ran back inside for the rest of the animals.

By now, the music had stopped and the audience's grumbles echoed through the building. Haibu realized that all eyes were on her. She stood there, stunned.

To her dismay, standing in the middle of the circus ring was the ringmaster with two of his workers.

They were holding Scotty, who was squirming like mad. They were caught.

The rescue could be foiled.

"Your little game is over, child! Give me back my animals and I won't have my elephant crush this boy's head," growled the ringmaster.

But Haibu was no longer afraid. She had had enough. She was lost, far from her family, and had gone toe-to-toe with a polar bear. She was not going to back down from this cruel circus man.

She marched toward the men.

"Haibu, don't!" shouted Wiz. "These men have no hearts! I can't let you two get hurt! Think of yourselves and the other animals!"

Haibu kept her eyes on the ringmaster as she yelled back to Wiz, "I *am* thinking of the animals." She picked up the microphone and spoke to the ringmaster. "If you hurt him, I will show my hunting skills one last time, and you will be the prey!"

The ringmaster looked around as if searching for someone to help him.

Haibu continued, "People of New York City, we need your help. The animals you watched

performing here today did not want to perform for you. They were forced to perform those tricks. They were whipped and starved until they did whatever these men wanted them to do. For each trick, it takes years of abuse for the animal to perform it correctly. If the animals are able to have young, their babies are immediately ripped away from them and sold to another circus." She paused for the audience to take in what she said. "These are living creatures. They feel pain, just like we do. They feel stressed when they are locked up, just like we do."

The crowd hung on every word Haibu said. She knew this was her moment.

"Can't you hear the animals cry out when they get whipped? The animals cry because it hurts them. They cry because it's painful and they don't want to do tricks anymore. They just want to be able to live and love, just like all of us. This elephant here, his name is Wiz. He can't even stand up in his own cage."

Feeling the courage, Haibu walked closer to the crowd. "Here is what is really sad. When this show is over, you are free to go home to your families and loved ones. When this show is over, these animals have to go back to their cages, chained up and whipped if they take too long to get back in there."

Haibu's voice quivered. "While you sleep peacefully at night, millions of them are crying and can't understand why no one will help them. They're dying inside. I've seen enough and I am going to be the change for these animals! And if I can do this at ten years old, what's your excuse for not helping as well?"

She dropped the mic and stared at the audience.

The crowd stood and cheered and stomped for Haibu. They began yelling at the ringmaster. Faced with the angry crowd, the ringmaster and workers panicked and let go of Scotty. He made a break for the front door.

"Haibu, run!" he yelled.

Haibu raced toward the door, shouting, "Wiz, follow me! Nanuqs—I mean bears—this way!"

The circus workers and animals began running for the front door. Zeek held it open.

"Let's go! Come on!"

The bears flew past everyone, including Zeek.

Again, he closed his eyes and said a quick prayer. "Nice bears, you don't want to eat little ole Zeek, do you?"

Scotty followed the bears out and jumped up into the truck.

Not quite out of the arena yet, Haibu was running just ahead of the ringmaster. He tried to grab her, snapping his whip above his head.

"You don't like animals being whipped, do you? Well, since you scared them all off, it looks like you will be getting it instead!" He had Haibu in his sights, and she could hear the snaps of his whip.

Seeing the ringmaster about to whip Haibu, Wiz galloped toward her and lashed out with his trunk, hitting the ringmaster and knocking him to the ground unconscious. Seeing the circus workers still chasing them, Wiz galloped toward the front door at full speed with Haibu following close behind.

"Haibu, tell your friend at the door to *moooooooove*!"

"Move, Zeek!" Haibu shouted.

Zeek's eyes were as big as bowling balls. He was face to face with a five-ton elephant—and it was barreling right for him, with no emergency brakes.

"EEEEEEEEEEE!" That was Zeek, screaming at the highest pitch ever produced by a male.

Scotty acted quickly to tackle Zeek, knocking him away from the door.

Wiz stopped the only way he could. He slid his entire body forward as if he was sliding into home plate and crashed halfway through the front door becoming stuck.

"Hurry, Haibu! Crawl under me!" Wiz commanded. Haibu slid around his belly and through his legs and out the front door. Wiz squatted down so the front entrance was completely blocked.

About to jump in the truck, Haibu looked back to see that Wiz was stuck. She ran back and pulled his trunk. "Push, Wiz! We have to go!"

"Haibu, stop," Wiz said.

"We don't have time! Push!"

Wiz shook his trunk enough to knock Haibu backward.

"Haibu, go now!"

"I'm not leaving you!"

"Go! There is no time. The other animals need

your help!"

With tears running down her cheeks, Haibu pleaded again, "Please, they will kill you if you stay!"

Wiz smiled at Haibu, "None of that matters, little Haibu. What's important is that those animals are my friends and they will finally be able to live a real life. And it is all because of you."

"We can't leave without you! No, Wiz. Please!"

Scotty and Zeek grabbed Haibu from behind and carried her back to the truck.

"I will never forget you, Haibu."

Haibu was still screaming. "No! Wiz! No!"

Eron walked into the light from the back of the trailer. "Goodbye, old friend."

"Goodbye, Eron. Take care of Haibu, she will need you," Wiz said.

As the truck door shut, Wiz could still hear Haibu screaming his name.

"Wiz, pleeeeaaaaaase!"

"Goodbye, Haibu," he whispered.

The workers inside were yelling at Wiz. Then there was the cracking of the whip. Over and over.

HOME

Word of Haibu and her friends freeing the circus animals traveled quickly. They were the top news story throughout the world media, appearing on every major news channel. You couldn't walk by a newsstand anywhere in the United States and not see a picture of Haibu. It didn't take long for her parents in Montooka to get the news that their daughter was safe and sound in New York City.

The governor held a dinner for the kids and presented them with the Key to the City. In addition, he outlawed the use of animals in any circus that came to the state of New York. He also arranged for a chartered plane to fly Haibu and her friend Kanuux back to Montooka.

Scotty, Zeek, Ollie, and Haibu gathered on the tarmac next to the plane. "Well, I guess this is goodbye. For now," Haibu said. The boys nodded.

"You sure you have to go? I think you should stay," Scotty said with a hopeful smile.

"I do. It's my home."

Haibu hugged Zeek, "Zeek, you were so brave. Thank you for helping the animals. For that, I want you to keep the Key to the City."

Zeek smiled from ear to ear. "Thanks, Haibu! This is awesome!"

Haibu hugged Ollie next. "Ollie, you were like a captain of a ship, so I got you this." Haibu pulled a book from her bag, titled *Noah's Ark*. "It's kind of popular. Just sayin'."

Ollie took the book and gave her a big hug back. "Thanks, Haibu."

Last was Scotty. "Scotty, what I thought was the worst thing to happen in my life has turned out to be the best thing, because I met you. I will return, but until I do, I want you to have this."

Haibu removed the Shookia from her wrist and tied it around Scotty's. "It's so you don't forget me."

"I won't forget you, Haibu," Scotty replied, trying to catch his tears before she saw them. They embraced in a long hug.

"Haibu," Zeek interrupted. "We pitched in to get you something, too." He reached into his pocket and pulled out a thick gold chain with a nameplate that

said *WIZ*.

Haibu carefully hung the heavy chain around her neck.

"It's not real gold, but maybe one day," Scotty said.

Haibu rubbed her finger across the nameplate. "Wiz, we will never forget you. Maybe when I come back we can free you once and for all"

And after one last group hug, the boys watched as Haibu's plane disappeared into the distance.

♥

NEVER "THE END"

HAIBU WILL BE BACK . . .

AN INTERVIEW WITH HAIBU

What's your favorite animal?
Haibu: ALL of them!

Where are you originally from?
Haibu: Montooka.

What's your favorite color?
Haibu: Yellow. Like my favorite food popcorn!

What do you want to be when you grow up?
Haibu: The Animal Protector, of course!

If you could have any superpower what would it be?
Haibu: Since I can already talk to animals… maybe being able to turn invisible whenever I want.

Who is your best friend? Is it your pet Kanuux?
Haibu: He's not my pet, he is a wild animal—but yes, he is my best friend! He is terrific at cuddling too.

Cookies or Cupcakes?

Haibu: That's a tough one! If I had to choose one, I would say cookies with cupcake frosting on it. Mmm!

Where in the world would you like to visit?

Haibu: Australia, for sure! I have always wanted to hop like a kangaroo with an actual kangaroo!

What do you look to for inspiration?

Haibu: My Shookia. It is my bracelet that reminds me that I can achieve anything I want, as long as I work hard and am true to myself!

What's your favorite activity to do when you're not saving animals?

Haibu: I like having game nights with my family. Even though my brother can be annoying, sometimes he can be A LOT of fun!

What's your biggest fear?

Haibu: I'm scared of the dark but I have a cool elephant nightlight.

What advice would you give other kids?

Haibu: Always stand up and be the voice for others who don't have one. Be kind and treat everyone with compassion and empathy. Be Happy. Be Friendly. Be Family.

AUTHOR'S NOTE

The life stories of the creator and developers of Haibu are similar to the tales of misfits. We aren't perfect, nor do we claim to be. Our individual journeys brought us together to create something beautiful and bring a much-needed voice to animals everywhere. This is how Haibu was born.

For us, Haibu is about helping humanity understand the plight of all living creatures with whom we share our planet. We aspire to instill permanent change in the thought and value systems of future generations regarding the global treatment of wild animals and the preservation of our planet.

Although there are many topics that need addressing—like the rate of animal extinction, deforestation, climate change, marine conservation, and more—this story focuses on animal captivity in the circus.

From the outside, a circus looks like fun for the whole family, with spectacular tricks performed by animals and humans alike. But if you pulled back the curtain, you would discover that the reality is much more sinister than that. The animals are left alone, chained up, and beaten into submission in order to learn the tricks. There is a lot more work to be done so that these circuses stop using animals as entertainment.

If this book provoked children to question our societal standards, gave them a sense of compassion and desire to learn more and get involved, we have accomplished our goal.

What matters is not what you've done, but what you do going forward. Leave your politics out of it and your heart in it. Haibu is a story for everyone.

"When children learn about wildlife and begin loving all the magnificent creatures they will forever fight to protect them. Haibu will lead the children on this important journey with a vital purpose." —John Baker, Chief Program Officer/Managing Director at WildAid

WILDAID

All around the world, populations of many vulnerable wildlife species are devastated by poaching for commercial trade. Shark fin, elephant ivory, rhino horn, tiger bones, and pangolin scales are just some of the products some people buy.

We believe that when the buying stops, the killing can too.

The illegal wildlife trade is a multi-billion-dollar global industry largely driven by consumer demand in expanding economies. While most wildlife conservation groups focus on scientific studies and anti-poaching efforts, WildAid works to reduce global consumption of wildlife products and to increase local support for conservation efforts.

We also work with governments and partners to protect fragile marine reserves from illegal fishing and shark finning, to enhance public and political will for anti-poaching efforts, and to reduce climate change impacts.

We believe that when people become aware of the realities associated with these products, most will stop buying them.

WildAid conducts awareness campaigns aimed at persuading people to stop buying these products. Reducing the demand is a critical long-term solution to widespread wildlife poaching.

BLAKE FREEMAN grew up in many midwestern states but lived the majority of his life in Nashville, Tennessee. Since relocating to Los Angeles, he has been in the entertainment business for over 12 years as an actor, director, writer, and producer of film and television. The books he read as a child shaped his view of the world. With that in mind, he has always felt that wild animals need a voice, and therefore Haibu was created.

TARA PRICE was born in Ann Arbor, Michigan, and now lives in Los Angeles, California. She has experience in everything from sales and IT to acting and production. Tara is also the voice of Haibu; any time you hear Haibu speak on YouTube, television, or in her upcoming feature film, it's Tara's voice!